William Kotzwinkle and Glenn Murray

Walter the Farting Dog
Trouble at the Yard Sale

Illustrated by Audrey Colman

PUFFIN BOOKS

PUFFIN BOOKS
Published by the Penguin Group
Penguin Young Readers Group, 345 Hudson Street, New York, New York 10014, U.S.A.
Penguin Group (Canada), 90 Eglinton Avenue East, Suite 700, Toronto, Ontario, Canada M4P 2Y3
(a division of Pearson Penguin Canada Inc.)
Penguin Books Ltd, 80 Strand, London WC2R ORL, England
Penguin Ireland, 25 St Stephen's Green, Dublin 2, Ireland
(a division of Penguin Books Ltd)
Penguin Group (Australia), 250 Camberwell Road, Camberwell, Victoria 3124, Australia
(a division of Pearson Australia Group Pty Ltd)
Penguin Books India Pvt Ltd, 11 Community Centre, Panchsheel Park, New Delhi - 110 017, India
Penguin Group (NZ), Cnr Airborne and Rosedale Roads, Albany, Auckland 1310,
New Zealand (a division of Pearson New Zealand Ltd)
Penguin Books (South Africa) (Pty) Ltd, 24 Sturdee Avenue, Rosebank, Johannesburg 2196, South Africa

Registered Offices: Penguin Books Ltd, 80 Strand, London WC2R ORL, England

First published in the United States of America by Dutton, a division of Penguin Young Readers Group, 2004
Published by Puffin Books, a division of Penguin Young Readers Group, 2006

1 3 5 7 9 10 8 6 4 2

Text copyright © William Kotzwinkle and Glenn Murray, 2004
Illustrations copyright © Audrey Colman, 2004
All rights reserved

Designed by Jason Henry

CIP Data is available.

Puffin Books ISBN 0-14-240626-0

Manufactured in China

For everyone who's ever felt
misjudged or misunderstood

All the other tables at the big yard sale were crowded with customers.
"We haven't sold a thing," said Father. "Nobody even comes near us."
Walter farted. He was happy to be here even if nobody bought anything.

Betty and Billy were bored. "Can we go get some ice cream?"

"Get one for me," said Father.

Betty said, "We'll get one for you too, Walter."

Walter farted happily.

"I'll mark everything down to a nickel," said Father to Walter. But still nobody came near their table.

   I wonder why? asked Walter, farting thoughtfully.

   Finally, a man came over to Father's table.

"How's business?"

"Terrible," said Father.

   Walter farted.

"Interesting dog," said the man. "Is he for sale?"

   Father looked slowly around to see if Betty and Billy were near.

   "Ten dollars," said Father.

   Walter looked at Father. *But I'm the family dog! I'm your friend!*

   "Leash included," said Father.

When Betty and Billy returned, Father was counting the money the man had given him.

"Where's Walter?" they asked.

Father looked around. "Oh, he must have wandered off. He'll be back."

Father ate his ice cream. Then he ate Walter's.

Betty and Billy ran through the neighborhood, calling,
"Walter, where are you?"

Walter was fastened to a fart-catcher.

"You're going to blow up this balloon," said his new owner.
"Get busy."

Walter felt awful. *Betty! Billy! Where are you?* He couldn't move.
All he could do was fart. The balloon inflated.

"Now another one."

Walter farted. The second balloon inflated.

"You've got fifteen more to go. Eat your beans."

While Walter tooted, the man got dressed in a clown suit. "It's for a children's party," said the clown.

Well, at least it's for children, thought Walter, and farted. Another balloon inflated.

"Walter," called Betty and Billy. "We miss you!"

Walter missed them too. But all he could do was eat beans and blow up balloons.

"It's for a good cause," said the clown.

When all the balloons were inflated, he gathered them up.

Don't leave me! barked Walter.

But he was stuck in the fart-catcher. And the clown was gone.

Downtown, a security guard was surprised to see a clown enter the bank, carrying a big bunch of balloons.

"Going to make a deposit?" asked the guard, smiling.

"Deposit this." The clown handed the guard a balloon.

"Thanks," said the guard.

"You're welcome," said the clown, and stuck a pin in the balloon.

The balloon popped. A rush of gas hit the guard, and he sank to the floor. The clown laughed behind his big red nose. It was a secret gas mask.

He turned to some nearby customers and popped another balloon.
The customers sank to the floor.

"Give me the money," the clown yelled, waving his bunch of balloons, "or I'll pop every one of them."

"Give him what he wants," choked the bank manager, tears streaming down his face.

The clown grabbed the sack of money and backed out the door. He jumped into his Fun-mobile and made his escape.

WANTED
for Bank Robbery

artist composite

walter was finishing the last of the beans when the door flew open and the clown came in. He dropped the sack of money on the floor and turned on the TV.

"Today," said the announcer, "a bank robber dressed as a clown used an unknown gas to get away with a fortune."

"Nice work, partner," said the clown to walter.

With a sinking feeling, walter realized he'd been farting his heart out for crime. Not for a children's party. Not for a good cause.

The clown lit a fifty-dollar cigar. "You'll have the best beans money can buy."

He opened a fresh bag of balloons and attached them to the fart-catcher. "Get busy, Fart-face. I'm robbing another bank tomorrow."

The clown reached up to adjust the first balloon. "I smell a leak," he said.
The glowing end of his cigar met the stream of escaping gas.

The fart-catcher exploded. Walter was launched across the room.
The clown was blown through the TV screen.

Walter snatched up the sack of money.
With his tail still smoking, he ran for home.

Hundred-dollar bills fluttered behind him.

"He's back!" cried Betty and Billy, opening the door.

"We're rich," cried Father, clutching fistfuls of money.

"You're under arrest," said a policeman. He had followed the trail of bills across town.

Walter tugged at the policeman's sleeve.

"He wants you to follow him," said Mother.

Walter led the police back to the clown's hideout.
The clown was trying to pull himself out of the TV set
when they snapped on the handcuffs.

"Good dog," said Father.

"Great dog," said the policeman.

"Careful with those balloons," said the other policeman.

They threw a big party for Walter.

"We all feel safer with Walter among us," said the bank manager.

"He's a true hero for our time," said the mayor.

The crowd cheered, and Walter farted.

"No one could be more proud than we are," said Father. "Proud to call Walter our very own."